THE HUTCHINSON
BOOK OF
DOG
TALES

HUTCHINSON

London Sydney Auckland Johannesburg

THE HUTCHINSON BOOK OF DOG TALES
A HUTCHINSON BOOK 0 09 189324 0

Published in Great Britain by Hutchinson,
an imprint of Random House Children's Books

This edition published 2004

1 3 5 7 9 10 8 6 4 2

RANDOM HOUSE CHILDREN'S BOOKS
61–63 Uxbridge Road, London W5 5SA
A division of The Random House Group Ltd

RANDOM HOUSE AUSTRALIA (PTY) LTD
20 Alfred Street, Milsons Point, Sydney,
New South Wales 2061, Australia

RANDOM HOUSE NEW ZEALAND LTD
18 Poland Road, Glenfield, Auckland 10, New Zealand

RANDOM HOUSE (PTY) LTD
Endulini, 5A Jubilee Road, Parktown 2193, South Africa

THE RANDOM HOUSE GROUP Limited Reg. No. 954009
www.kidsatrandomhouse.co.uk

A CIP catalogue record for this book is available from the British Library.

Printed in Hong Kong

Contents

Piper

Emma Chichester Clark

When Piper was a little puppy his mother used to say to him, "Always obey your master. Always look both ways when you cross the road. And always help anyone in danger."

Once Piper was old enough to leave home Mr Jones, his new master, came to take him away. He was a strange, fierce-looking man and Piper felt nervous.

"Don't worry," said Piper's mother comfortingly. "If you remember the three things I told you, you will be a good dog and I shall always be proud of you."

Mr Jones dragged Piper up a hill to the lonely crooked house where he lived. "Tomorrow I want you to take care of the rabbits in my vegetable patch. Teach them a lesson they won't forget!" said Mr Jones grimly.

I can obey that command easily, thought Piper.

He worked very hard. He took good care of the
rabbits all day and by the evening he had
taught them to jump over him.
They had a lovely time.

But Mr Jones was furious.
He came up behind
Piper and hit him with
a big stick. "You stupid
disobedient dog!" he
snarled. "You were meant
to get rid of the rabbits!
Stay in this hut until
I decide what to do
with you."

He tied poor Piper up, without any food.

But the rabbits didn't forget Piper. They
visited him every night and brought
him their food. Piper
thought they
were very
kind, though
he didn't
enjoy eating
lettuce.

A week later Mr Jones bought a new dog. It was a vicious creature with teeth like knives.

"Brutus will get rid of all the rabbits," said Mr Jones.

"And then he will teach you how to be a real dog!"

Brutus growled at Piper and bared his sharp teeth.

Piper was terrified.

That night Piper bit through the rope and escaped.

He ran and ran through dark woods.

He ran up and down steep hills.

And he plunged across a river.

At last he came to a great city. It was dark and noisy. The houses were like grey boxes. Everywhere cars and trucks hurried by.

Piper looked both ways and tried to cross the road. But the traffic never stopped. He felt very small and alone.

Then Piper saw an old lady standing on the other side of the street. She called to him and he gave a friendly bark in return.

Suddenly she stepped out towards him into the road without looking! A car was about to run her over! Piper darted in front of her and stopped the car.

But the old lady was so startled she fell backwards onto the pavement. She lay there without moving.

Soon a crowd gathered and an ambulance arrived.

The ambulance men gently lifted the old
lady onto a stretcher
and took her away.

Piper was miserable.
Nobody noticed him sitting
there, so he crept away.

Piper had banged his leg
on the car when he saved
the old lady. He limped
sadly along until he came
to a park.

It began to rain. His leg hurt very much so he hid under a bush.

As he drifted off to sleep, Piper dimly heard voices through the raindrops drumming on the leaves.

Suddenly there was a loud shout nearby. "I've found him!"

Piper felt himself being gently lifted up and wrapped in a warm blanket. Then he fell asleep. He did not understand that everyone had been looking for the brave dog who had saved the old lady's life.

When he woke up he was lying on a soft sofa with a bowl of delicious food in front of him. And there was the old lady smiling at him! "You are a hero," she said.

"I'd like you to live with me," said the old lady. "But first I have to put up notices to say that I have found you, in case your owner wants you back. If no one claims you after a week then you can stay."

FOUND

Black dog, v. thin,
long tail.
Owner please ring
352794
within seven days
if wanted.

Piper couldn't explain that he never wanted to see his cruel owner again.

Every day he waited in case Mr Jones called.

By the end of the week he was so tired he fell asleep beside the telephone.

Suddenly it rang!

The old lady lifted the receiver and Piper heard Mr Jones's grating voice: "That black dog is mine, but you are welcome to him. He is such a coward he won't even chase a rabbit!"

"I should hope not, you horrible man," said the old lady in a shocked voice, and she put the receiver down with a bang.

"How lucky I am to have found you," she said. "Now we can both look after each other."

Jake

Deborah King

Early morning had never been Jake's favourite time of day.
He preferred to wake up slowly and take things easy.

But today was different. Jake had a very good reason for
getting up.

Grandpa was coming, and they were going to the beach.

But when Jake looked downstairs, Grandpa wasn't there!

That's funny, thought Jake. I wonder if he's in the garden? But he couldn't find Grandpa anywhere.

"He's never been this late," he whined. "Surely he can't have forgotten me."

Jake couldn't bear to wait a minute longer. The sun was shining and somehow he'd got to find Grandpa. He slipped quietly through the back door and was on his way.

At the end of the lane he met a party of schoolchildren running down to the beach. I wonder if they've seen Grandpa, thought Jake.

But the children just wanted to play, and soon Jake was too busy with his head under water to think about Grandpa.

Dripping wet by now, and rather bedraggled, Jake stumbled up the beach and bumped straight into some grown-ups.

They're sure to have seen Grandpa, he thought.

But for some reason they weren't at all helpful.

Jake was in trouble now.

All alone, and wishing he'd stayed in bed after all, Jake suddenly had an idea. "Perhaps if I bark really loud Grandpa will hear me and come to my rescue."

Everyone in the whole world heard him, everyone except Grandpa.

It was the windsurfers who set him free. "Anything for a quiet life," they told him. But Jake wasn't listening.

"I'll show them a trick or two," he barked.

The windsurfers were soon bored with him. They picked up their sailboards and headed down to the sea. Jake went too. Perhaps Grandpa is taking his morning dip, he thought.

And before anyone could stop him, he was afloat!

"If I keep to the shallows," he barked, "Grandpa is bound to see me."

He didn't notice the wind getting up. In no time at all it was blowing him further and further out to sea.

He was going very fast.

TOO FAST!

SPLASH!

But Jake was rescued just in time.

As he was rowed across the bay, he barked as loud as he could, just in case Grandpa could hear him.

WOOF!   WOOF!   WOOF!

A young man in a yacht recognized that bark only too well.

"Jake! What are you doing out here in the middle of the ocean?" he cried. "And where's your old friend?" Jake wished he knew.

"Well, you won't find him where we're going," continued the young man, hauling Jake aboard.

But Jake wasn't listening. Looking for Grandpa was turning into a great adventure.

Once ashore, Jake was so busy scrambling over cliffs and exploring the coves and rockpools that he almost forgot about Grandpa.

It was while he was lying in a pool that he suddenly remembered.

I suppose I'd better take a look, he thought.

But he was gone too long and he missed the boat.

There was nothing for it but a long cold swim.

As he paddled his way through the deep, murky water he came to the conclusion that looking for Grandpa hadn't been such a good idea after all.

It wasn't an easy ride home. The wind was blowing even harder and the boat rocked and rolled in the swell. "No use calling for Grandpa now," he sighed, and he hid down below. For once in his life he had nothing to say.

Not until he was safely ashore did Jake begin to feel like a real dog again. "It's good to be back on dry land!" he barked.

But it just wasn't the same without Grandpa and, shaking the sand from his eyes, Jake thought of one last place where Grandpa might be . . . the village pub.

But even the barman hadn't seen Grandpa. No one had.

Jake had finally run out of ideas.

It was time to call off the search and head for home.

However, Jake was in for a surprise. Who should be waiting for him, but Grandpa!

"Where have you been all day?" exclaimed his old friend. "Why didn't you wait for me this morning?"

All at once, Jake realized his mistake. And from that day on, he made up his mind never to get up too early, ever again.

And he never did!

I Hope You Know

Gina Wilson and Alison Catley

When I wake up . . . bring me a big juicy marrow bone.
  When I bark . . .
open the door, even
if it's wet or snowy.

When I pull at my lead . . . run like the wind.

When I stop dead . . .
you stop too.

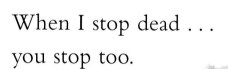

When I wag
my tail . . . pat me all over.

When I lie on my back with my feet in the air . . . tickle
my hairy tum.

When I lick your toes . . . laugh, long and loud.

When I chew the mat . . .

give me a biscuit instead.

When I sit up on my
hind legs and beg . . .
give me another one!

When I yawn . . .
pull out my basket.

When I close my eyes . . .

switch off the light.

And I hope you
know I'm your
best friend for ever.

Mr Bill and Clarence

Kay Gallwey

Mr Bill is a kitten with a smart ginger moustache and long whiskers. His fur is ginger and white. He has big green eyes and because he is a Manx kitten, he has only a short stumpy tail.

On the night Mr Bill arrived he was tucked into a box with teddy and a cosy cover.

But next morning, Mr Bill wasn't with teddy in the box,

or on the chair,

or on the sofa.

He was with Clarence
in his big basket.

Clarence is a big collie dog, with a long golden coat, big white ruff, soft dark ears and big brown eyes. Mr Bill loves him.

Mr Bill and Clarence have breakfast together.

Mr Bill tries a bit of
Clarence's lunch.
Clarence doesn't mind a bit.

They share a juicy bone for tea.

Mr Bill and Clarence love to play together.
They play jumping the sofa.

They play hide and seek.
Mr Bill loves to jump out and surprise Clarence.

Mr Bill hasn't got a
tail to play with,

so he borrows Clarence's.

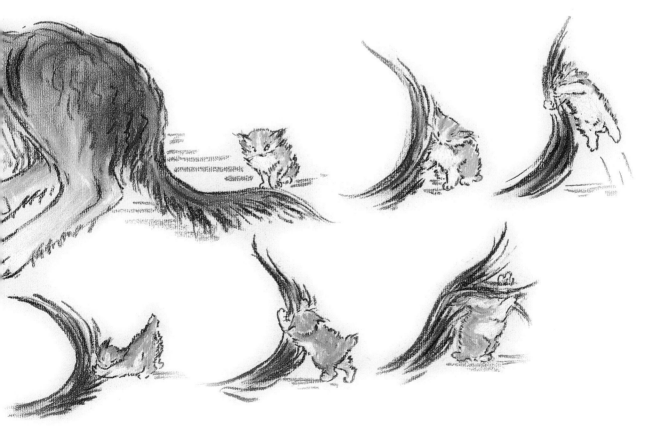

Mr Bill grows and grows.
But he still borrows Clarence's tail.

Clarence wants to borrow Mr Bill's cat door,
but he is too big.

Clarence and Mr Bill go for walks in summer.

Mr Bill and Clarence go
for walks in winter.

Every night, Mr Bill
washes himself,

then he washes Clarence.

Then they curl up together in their big basket, and go to sleep. It's a bit of a squash, but they don't mind a bit.

Clever Dog, Kip!

Benedict Blathwayt

Clever Dog, Kip! 🦴 Benedict Blathwayt

> Hurry up, Fudge.
> I've got a busy day ahead.

Clever Dog, Kip! — Benedict Blathwayt

Clever Dog, Kip! 🦴 Benedict Blathwayt

Hurry up! We must get the bales in.

Kip!

Doodle Dog

Frank Rodgers

Sam was playing with his toys on the kitchen table. Five cars, four spacemen, three cowboys, two Indians and a small teddy bear called Ned. His mum was chopping carrots for the soup.

Suddenly Sam looked up. "Mum, could I have a dog? A real dog, I mean," he said. "Please," he added, before his mum had to remind him.

"I'm sorry, Sam," she said. "A flat isn't the right sort of place to keep a dog. We're five floors up and we've no garden. It wouldn't be kind."

"What about a very small dog. A really tiny one?" Sam asked hopefully.

"Not even a Chihuahua," smiled his mum. "And that kind of dog is so small it can sit in a teacup . . . just like Ned!" Sam wasn't sure that he liked the idea of a dog in a teacup.

Sam opened one of his books and pointed to a picture. "That's the kind of dog I want," he said.

His mum looked at the picture. A bright, little, black, brown and white puppy sat in a farmyard.

Sam's mum smiled. "He is nice," she said.

"He wouldn't fit in a teacup," said Sam. "But if he were mine, I could teach him to do some tricks . . . shake hands, fetch a stick, balance a biscuit on his nose and catch a ball in mid-air. And he could sleep at the bottom of my bed."

His mum nodded. "Perhaps we'll get a dog if we move house," she said. "Now why don't you get out your crayons and draw a dog, Sam?"

"Do you like my dog, Mum?" said Sam, a few minutes later.

"Well done," said his mother. "It's very good!"

Sam frowned. "It's all right, I suppose," he said, "but will you help me draw a better one?"

His mother laughed. "I'm not very good at drawing, Sam, but I'll try," she said.

She sat beside Sam and helped him to sketch the outline of a dog. "I'm afraid this is only a doodle," she said.

"Doodle," said Sam. "That's a good name for a dog. Doodle dog. I'm going to call him Doodle."

"Why don't you colour him in?" his mum suggested.

"All right," said Sam. And he gave Doodle black ears, a black tail, some brown patches and a spotty tummy.

"He's lovely!" exclaimed his mum when Sam had finished. "He looks so friendly!"

"He looks like a real dog," said Sam.

Sam liked Doodle so much that he put the drawing on the bed beside him before he went to sleep.

"Goodnight, Doodle," he whispered.

Next morning Sam was woken by a tickly feeling on his cheek. He opened his eyes and stared in amazement. Doodle was licking his face!

"Is it really you, Doodle!" he laughed, struggling to sit up.

"Wuff, yip!" barked Doodle, and Sam knew that he meant, "Of course!"

Sam was so pleased that he gave Doodle an enormous hug. Doodle wagged his tail. He liked Sam.

Sam jumped out of bed and started to put on his clothes.
"Can you do tricks, Doodle?" he asked eagerly.

Doodle jumped off the bed and stood on his hind legs.
He looked up at Sam as if to say, "What do you think of
that, eh?"

Sam laughed. "You are just the kind of dog
I've always wanted!" he said. "Can you
do other tricks?"

Sam picked up a small
rubber ball and carefully
put it on Doodle's nose.

Not only did Doodle balance the ball, he tossed his head so that the ball bounced right up to the ceiling. As it came back down he jumped and caught it neatly in his mouth. Then he gave the ball back to Sam.

"Hurray!" shouted Sam. "You're the best dog in the world. Shake hands!"

Doodle lifted up his paw and solemnly shook hands with Sam.

"You're so clever. Bet you'd make a good sheepdog," said Sam. "Come and see my farm."

Sam went to his toy box and took out his farmyard set. He arranged the fence posts in a square and put the little wooden animals inside.

He pushed open the tiny gate and grinned at Doodle. "This is our farm, Doodle," he smiled. "Let's go in."

Sam and Doodle stood in the middle of the farmyard. All around them they could hear the sounds of the farm. Hens clucking and cows mooing. Ducks quacking and pigs grunting.

But the noisiest of all were the sheep. They had pushed the gate open and run out of their field. They were wandering all over the farmyard bleating loudly and eating the flowers from the farmhouse window boxes.

"Quick, Doodle," said Sam. "Let's round up the sheep."

"Yep!" barked Doodle, which, of course, meant "Yes!"

Doodle was a wonderful sheepdog. He dashed here and there.

Sometimes sneaking up behind the sheep, wriggling along on his tummy,

sometimes darting quickly.

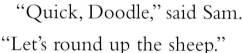

With Sam's help he soon managed to herd all the sheep back into their field.

Sam closed the gate. "Whew!" he said in relief. "Nice work, Doodle!"

Doodle wagged his tail and barked at Sam. "Grrrif, yap, yap, rruff!" which meant, "Now let's explore the farm!"

Together Sam and Doodle had a lovely time. They saw the hens and their chicks, the ducks on the pond, the cows in their field of clover, the pigs in their sty, and even the nanny-goat in its pen.

They smelled the warm summer smells of the country and Sam
threw sticks for Doodle to fetch. Then they went into the barn.

Inside, the air was warm and still, and little shafts of sunlight
flickered through gaps in the wooden slats.

The hay loft was filled with big square bales of yellow hay.

At the bottom of the ladder was a pile of loose hay. "Let's get to work," laughed Sam.

Sam lifted big armfuls of hay and Doodle helped by pushing the bits and pieces into piles with his nose.

Soon the barn looked neat and tidy.

"Grr, woof, yap! That was fun!" barked Doodle.

And from the corner of the barn, as if in answer, they heard a soft, "Neigh . . ."

Sam and Doodle looked round. There, in the shadows, stood a beautiful chestnut pony.

It neighed again as if to say, "Here I am. Come and talk to me."

Sam picked up a handful of hay and went over to feed the pony.

"You were so quiet," laughed Sam as he stroked the pony's nose, "we didn't notice you!"

The pony nodded its head and gently took the hay from Sam's outstretched hand. Sam giggled as the velvety nose tickled him.

"Breakfast time, Sam," called his mother.

"Coming, Mum!" Sam answered.

"Come on, Doodle," he said. "Let's go."

Doodle didn't answer. Sam looked down. Doodle had gone, but his picture was on the floor.

"Come on, Doodle, I'll carry you," Sam said, picking up the drawing.

And as Sam walked towards the kitchen, he looked at the drawing and smiled.

"That was great fun, Doodle," he said.

"Let's go to the park after breakfast."

Hangdog

Graham Round

Hangdog was the loneliest dog in the world. Although he was gentle
and kind and very polite, he just couldn't seem to make friends
however hard he tried.

Just one friend would do, Hangdog often thought; someone to come to tea. Every day he got out his best china and set the table for two. But no one ever came.

Sometimes he would stand in front of the mirror and try to work out what was wrong. "Maybe it's my growly voice," he said. "Or maybe I'm too fat. Or perhaps my face is too sad." But in the end he had to admit he was just a plain old hangdog that nobody liked.

One day it rained and rained. The city was dark and cold and full of puddles. Hangdog put on his raincoat and wandered down to the docks. As he looked out to sea he felt lonelier than ever.

Watching the boats bob about on the waves gave Hangdog an idea. "I'll build myself a boat and sail away to sea," he said. "There must be a friend for me somewhere in the world."

Back at home, Hangdog searched for something that would make a boat. In the corner of the shed stood an old grandfather clock.

He pulled it down from its dusty corner. The insides had all gone, but it had a happy face with a big smile.

"A grandfather boat," said Hangdog. "Perfect!"

A broomstick made a very good mast. An old tablecloth made a sail. A coal shovel made an excellent rudder.

Hangdog collected all the things he would need for his journey: some tins of marrowbone jelly, a rubber bone, a compass, a pair of binoculars and an umbrella in case it rained.

At last the boat was ready. Hangdog trundled it down to the shore.

No one noticed as the wind took up the tablecloth sail and blew the little grandfather boat out to sea.

A whole day passed. Soon Hangdog could see nothing but sea for miles and miles. He sniffed the salty air. He was all alone, but he didn't feel lonely at all.

That night, the sky grew dark and stormy. It began to rain and the waves rocked the little boat to and fro. This *is* exciting, thought Hangdog.

But as the night wore on the storm grew worse; the waves grew bigger and bigger and the wind grew stronger and stronger. A huge wave swept Hangdog overboard.

All night long, Hangdog hung on bravely to the mast. At last the storm passed and morning came. Hangdog looked around him, but there was no sign of the little grandfather boat.

Suddenly, a huge jet of water shot into the air.

What now? thought Hangdog.

A great whale rose out of the water. It opened its enormous mouth.

"Hello," said Hangdog. But just like everyone else, the whale didn't even notice him.

Hangdog swam on. Soon a faint outline appeared on the horizon. Was that land ahead?

It was. Hangdog doggy-paddled furiously, and soon he reached the shore of a desert island. He was so tired he lay down and fell asleep. All night long he slept on the sand, dreaming of storms and waves and boats and whales.

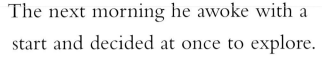

The next morning he awoke with a start and decided at once to explore. He walked up the beach and into a strange jungle world. He had never seen anything like it before. As he wandered deeper and deeper into the jungle he had the curious feeling that he was being watched. Suddenly, a huge tiger leapt out of the bushes.

"Oh, dear," cried Hangdog. He turned and ran, and with a great roar the tiger came after him.

Tiger chased Hangdog. What a chase! Hangdog ran and ran and ran until he came to a clearing. He looked right and he looked left, but there was nowhere else to run.

The tiger flashed out of the trees.

"Oh well," said Hangdog, "you may as well eat me. No one will miss me and no one will care."

Drooling at the mouth, the huge tiger looked at Hangdog.

Then he gave Hangdog a great big slobbery kiss!

"Eat you!" he said. "Not likely! I've been so lonely here on my own, I've been waiting for a friend just like you." And Tiger hugged Hangdog as if he would never let him go.

"I knew there was a friend for me somewhere in the world," said Hangdog.

And that night Tiger got out his very best china and the two friends took tea together under the moon.

Fraser's Grump

Sue Heap

Fraser was in a grump.

So he headed off to his favourite tree wearing his dad's kagoul and his sister's knapsack.

And just as he sat down
Buster the dog came up
wagging his tail.

"Oh no!" sighed Fraser.
"Buster, you'd better be
quiet if you want to stay
under the tree with me."

But Buster didn't want
to stay under a tree
keeping quiet. Buster
wanted to bark.

So he went and
barked at the cat.

The cat hissed and went to join Fraser under the tree.

Buster barked at the
tortoise.

The tortoise got
up slowly and went
to join Fraser and
the cat under
the tree.

Buster barked
at the hen.

The hen stopped
pecking and went
to join Fraser and
the cat and the tortoise
under the tree.

Buster barked at the rabbit.
The rabbit leapt into the air and
went to join Fraser and
the cat and the tortoise
and the hen under
the tree.

Buster barked at the heron.
The heron hastily folded
his newspaper and went
to join Fraser and the
cat and the tortoise and
the hen and the rabbit
under the tree.

Up came Buster.

"Sssssh!" said Fraser.

But Buster wasn't barking.
He was carrying a letter.
The letter said:

Please come home Fraser. Lunch is ready. love Mum x
P.S. Dad needs his Kagoul!
P.P.S. Jane says you can keep her knapsack till Friday x.

Fraser yelled, "WOOF!" Buster wagged his tail. Fraser put the letter in his pocket.

"SSSSSSHH!" said the cat and the tortoise and the hen and the rabbit and the heron under the tree.

So Fraser and Buster very quietly went away from the tree.

Then very noisily raced each other home for lunch.

Heaven

Nicholas Allan

Early one morning Lily woke up to find
Dill the dog packing.

"Where're you going?" she asked.

"Up there," said Dill.

"Can I come too?"

"Er . . . not yet," said Dill.

"But I want you to play."

"I'll be late," said Dill.

"Late for what?"

"I'm being collected."

"Why can't I come too?"

"You have to be invited," said Dill.

"Who invited *you*?" asked Lily.

"Us," said the angels.

"Does Dill have to go *now*?" asked Lily.

"Now," said the angels.

"Can't he stay just ten minutes?"

"Well . . . five minutes,"
said the angels.

"Will you be away
long?" asked Lily.

"A long time," said Dill.

"But you might not like it up there."

"I *will* like it up there."

"You might not though."

"Of course I'll like it. It's heaven, isn't it?"

"Might not . . . What do you think it's like then? Up there?"

"Nice," said Dill.

"Yes, but what's it *like*?"

"What do *you* think it's like?"

"Well," said Lily. "In heaven there's a funfair where all the rides are free and you're never sick once.

And there's a whole island made of chocolate with ice-cream clouds and sweets in caves and the sea is made of Coke and you can eat all you want and YOU'RE NEVER SICK ONCE!"

"No, no, no, no, no," said Dill.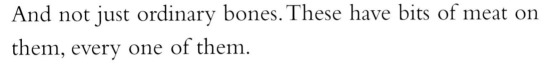

"It's not like that at all."

"Well, what is it like then?"

"Bones," said Dill.

"Bones?"

"Bones. All over the place. And not just ordinary bones. These have bits of meat on them, every one of them.

"And there are lampposts. Hundreds of them. And whiffy things to smell on the ground."

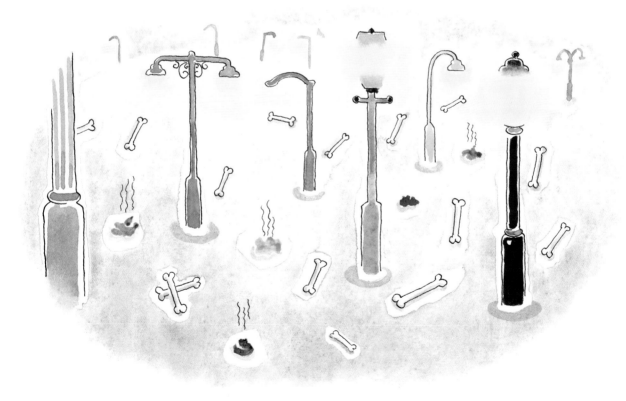

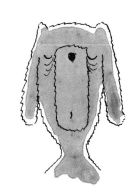

"YUCK!" said Lily. "Bones, lampposts, whiffy things. Doesn't sound like heaven to me."

"Nevertheless, that's what heaven's like."

"How do *you* know?" said Lily.

"How do you know it's not?" said Dill.

"Well, if it is, I wouldn't want to go there."

"Don't worry. You're not invited anyway."

"Wouldn't want to go anyway."

"Wouldn't want you there, thanks."

"Anyway, you might not go up – you might go DOWN," said Lily.

"Down?" said Dill.

"DOWN," said Lily.

"But I've always been a good dog," said Dill.

"What about that time you stole the chicken?"

"Well, apart from that," said Dill.

"What about the time you bit Aunt Julia?"

"Well, apart from that," said Dill.

"What about the time you . . . ?"

"All right, I've *tried* to be a good dog. OK?"

"Hmmph!" said Lily.

"Time," said the angel.

Lily walked home and went back to bed. When she woke up it was late. She ran downstairs and saw Dill's basket and his bowl and his scratches on the door and his lead and his yucky wet tennis ball.

She was very sad. Lily thought things would never be the same again.

But one day she met a stray puppy.

She took him home, and then began to remember all that Dill had said.

She took the puppy for a walk and found a street full of lampposts . . . and whiffy things and when they got home she gave him lots of bones – all with bits of meat on them.

He must think he's in
heaven already, thought Dill.

Winsome

Caroline Castle and Corrina Askin

Winsome was trotting home after a pleasant day
in the park, when . . .

Whoosh!

"You'll do!" said Dr Droge.

"Do for what?" said Winsome crossly.

"QUIET, you snivelling mutt!"
snapped Droge. And he threw
Winsome into the back of his van.

Winsome did not like the look
of Dr Droge one bit.

The van bumped along, tossing Winsome from side to side.

"Ouch, eeek! Oh! Steady on!" he cried.

But Droge did not slow down. Oh no. He went even faster.
Winsome was beginning to have a very bad feeling about Dr Droge.

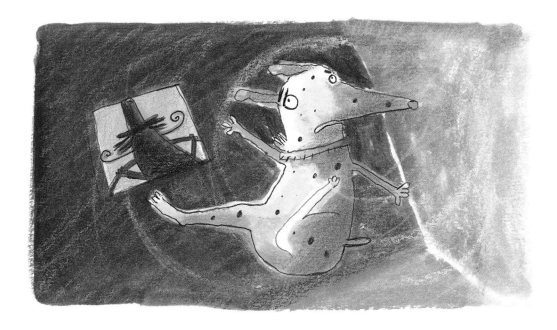

When the van stopped Winsome was hurled into a small cage at the back of a tent.

Inside were nine sad-looking little dogs.

"Hi, boys," said Winsome. "What's going on?"

Every one of the dogs looked as if it was the saddest day of their lives.

"Congratulations. You've joined the circus," said Dog Number Four. "We're Dr Droge's Doggie Troupe and now you're one of us."

"You're joking," said Winsome.

"I'm afraid not," said Dog Number Four. "And I'm sorry for you because that Droge is the biggest, cruellest master you'll ever meet."

"Hey, you poor mutts," said Winsome. "This is no life for a dog. What are we going to do about it?"

"There's nothing we can do," said Dog Number Five. "It's too dangerous."

"We'll see about that," said Winsome.

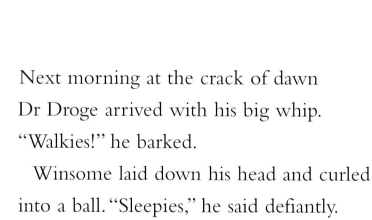

Next morning at the crack of dawn Dr Droge arrived with his big whip. "Walkies!" he barked.

Winsome laid down his head and curled into a ball. "Sleepies," he said defiantly.

"Oh, so, New Dog thinks he's clever, eh? Well, we'll soon knock him into shape."

And he cracked his whip a whisker away from Winsome's nose.

"OK, OK, hold your horses," said Winsome. "Walkies it is."

Walkies was not like
an ordinary walk for
an ordinary dog, in a
park or a wood. Oh no.
Dr Droge's walkies meant the
poor dogs running round and
round a big ring with the
whip cracking at their tails.
But worse was to come.

"Dress rehearsal," said Droge. Out of his pocket he took ten ghastly, pink ruffs.

"Ugh!" said Winsome. "I hope you're not expecting me to wear *that*!"

"New Dog causing trouble again?" said Droge, with a mean look in his eye.

"Firstly," said Winsome, "my name is Winsome. Secondly . . ."

But Droge was not listening. He grabbed Winsome by the scruff of his neck and tied on his ruff so tight that he could hardly breathe.

Winsome scrabbled at the ruff until he managed to work it loose. "Do I look stupid in this, or what?" he wheezed.

But worse was to come.

Droge lit a match and a small hoop burst into a blazing ring of fire.

"Dogs . . . JUMP!" he ordered.

"Oh, no!" said Winsome. "He's not expecting me to . . ."

" 'fraid so," said Number Four. "You'd better do what he says or, believe me, your life won't be worth living."

One by one the little dogs jumped through the flaming hoop.

Winsome could smell the dreadful whiff of singed fur. I hope that's not mine, he thought.

But worse was to come.

"Dogs . . . BEG!" barked Dr Droge.

One by one each little dog picked up a bowl and stood up on his hind legs.

"*One*, two, three! *One*, two, three!" barked Dr Droge, as they set off round the ring in time to the music.

"Now, this is the limit," said Winsome. "This is where I really put my paw down. Jumping through burning hoops is one thing, but begging . . .

"I won't do it!" said Winsome.

"What!" barked Dr Droge.

"There is no way that Winsome is begging," said Winsome firmly.

The other dogs stopped in their tracks, tails a-trembling. They all knew too well what Dr Droge did to troublemakers.

Dr Droge picked up Winsome by his tail and started hurling him about his head.

But Winsome did a great twist in midair and . . . bit Dr Droge on the bottom!

Dr Droge yelped in pain. He was beside himself. "That's it," he said, holding Winsome in a terrible grip. "I'm calling the police. Assaulting a world-famous dog trainer is a serious crime."

Unfortunately for Dr Droge a new Chief Inspector had just started that morning. "What's going on here, then?" the Chief Inspector snarled.

"This meddlesome mutt just bit me!" said Dr Droge, holding out Winsome by the throat.

The Chief Inspector did not look impressed. "Cruelty to small, innocent dogs is a serious crime," he said.

And Dr Droge was astonished to find himself arrested instead.

To their joy, the whole troupe was set free. They ran and jumped and sniffed and woofed for all they were worth.

"Thanks, Winsome," said Dog Number Three.

"No problem," said Winsome. "Just remember, when it looks like there's no way out, it's always worth having a go. You may lose some but you'll also . . ."

"Win some!" chorused the troupe.

"That's my name," said the little dog.

Acknowledgements

The publishers gratefully acknowledge the following authors and illustrators:

Piper published by Jonathan Cape Children's Books
Text and illustrations © Emma Chichester Clark, 1995

Jake published by Hutchinson Children's Books
Text and illustrations © Deborah King, 1988

I Hope You Know published by Hutchinson Children's Books
Text © Gina Wilson, 1989 Illustrations © Alison Catley, 1989

Mr Bill and Clarence published by The Bodley Head Children's Books
Text and illustrations © Kay Gallwey, 1990

Clever Dog, Kip! published by Julia MacRae Books as *Kip, A Dog's Day*
Text and illustrations © Benedict Blathwayt, 1996

Doodle Dog published by William Heinemann Ltd
Text and illustrations © Frank Rodgers, 1990

Hangdog published by Hutchinson Children's Books
Text and illustrations © Graham Round, 1987

Fraser's Grump published by Julia MacRae Books
Text and illustrations © Sue Heap, 1993

Heaven published by Hutchinson Children's Books
Text and illustrations © Nicholas Allan, 1996

Winsome
Text © Caroline Castle, 2004 Illustrations © Corrina Askin, 2004

With special thanks to Caroline Sheldon for her help with this anthology